Halloween in Hell

Halloween in Hell

Ashley Stoyanoff

Ashley Stoyanoff Books
London, Ontario

Halloween in Hell is a work of fiction. Names, characters, places,
and incidents are the products of the author's imagination or are
used fictitiously. Any resemblance to actual events, locales, or
persons, living or dead, is entirely coincidental.

Dedication

For Andrew.
You are a reason to smile and you give great hugs.
Never change.

I

Liv

Making a quiet entrance had never been his style, but crashing into a waitress and knocking a tray full of mugs out of her hands surely had to be an accident.

When the portal opened up in Witches Brew Coffee Shop, everyone, including the barista, stopped and stared. I was in a hurry, of course—there was only one coffee shop on this side of the campus. One coffee shop, one barista, one waitress, and you were lucky if there wasn't a lineup outside the door at any given time.

I looked up, sighing as Jaxon—my ex—materialized, stepping through the portal and grunting as he collided right into the back of a waitress. The tray in her hand teetered, before toppling over, the mugs shattering on the ceramic floor with a loud crash.

"Sorry, Lucy," Jaxon said, his rich voice carrying through the shop as he reached out, steadying the brunette, and then with a snap of his fingers, the tray was back in her hands, the mugs all back in one piece.

I watched him, frozen, because I just couldn't help myself. The man had always been worth looking at, even before I knew who he was. He had raven black hair, the cut, close cropped. He wasn't overly big, but he was muscular, and the perfect height. Not too tall, not too short. He was wearing a tee, black, with blue jeans, and a pair of kickass blue and black sneakers. And he was smiling. Dear Goddess, I loved that smile.

He turned toward me, his gaze hitting mine, and I felt my heart actually squeeze a little. Jaxon watched me in silence for a long moment, his smile slowly fading away, and then stepped toward me.

"Hey, Liv." He had a deep voice, warm and hard all mixed into one. The sound made me shiver. I wasn't sure if it was from excitement or dread.

Probably both.

My heart was pounding fast. I smiled, or I tried to, but it felt forced and unnatural. "Maybe next time you should try the door like a normal person," I said. I was kidding, but he didn't smile.

"I'm not exactly normal," he said seriously. "And I'm not exactly a person either."

That was true. He wasn't a person, exactly. Jaxon was a demon, but not just any demon. He was the son of the Devil, and the next in line to take over Hell.

"What are you doing here?" I asked, because he shouldn't have been here. He was supposed to be in Hell, training with the king himself.

"It's Monday." He took a few steps toward me, seemingly oblivious to the attention he was drawing, but I wasn't. People were staring. I could see it. Shit, I could almost feel it. Since his little secret came out a couple of months ago, the man couldn't go anywhere without people watching.

"Okay ..." I said, and then waited for him to elaborate. The line moved, and I moved with it. I was one person away from getting my mocha. I really needed that mocha.

When he only stood there staring at me, I waved an impatient hand. "And that's important why?"

He huffed and eyed me suspiciously. "It's Halloween and you haven't RSVP'd for my party yet."

I'd known it was coming, of course, but I'd let myself think that maybe he'd just not notice that I hadn't responded. Honestly, I'd been hoping he wouldn't clue in until it was too late.

I felt my heart rate pick up faster, and I hated myself for it. When the pumpkin colored envelope had appeared on my pillow last week, my first instinct was to say yes immediately. But then, as I ran a finger over his signature and thought about the night we broke up, my heart started to ache. So I'd tucked it away into my nightstand, and tried—hard—to pretend I never saw it.

"Party?" I folded my arms over my chest and pretended to think.

"Yeah, the Halloween party in Hell."

"Right, the party!" I snapped my fingers as though I'd forgotten all about it. "It must have slipped my mind."

He smiled—finally—that dimpled smile that always made my stomach clench. "Sure it did."

I laughed.

Jaxon didn't, although he did keep smiling.

"Um ... Please tell me you didn't drop by to personally collect my response."

"Of course I did."

I snorted. "A little desperate, don't you think?"

Another flash of dimples, and then he said, "It's a little late to play hard to get now, don't you think?"

He was just teasing, I knew it, but that didn't stop the heat from creeping up my neck and settling in my cheeks. I was certain I was as red as a tomato. I took a deep breath and glanced around. People were still staring, but that wasn't really a surprise. People always stared when the Prince of Hell was around.

"That was a mistake," I muttered, biting my bottom lip.

I glared at him and he stood there for a moment and stared, surprised, a little frown creasing his forehead. He took another step toward me, and reached out a hand, running his fingertips down the side of my face, along my jawline, before brushing his thumb across my lips. His touch sent a jolt through me and I froze, my eyes closing. "You don't mean that."

Another truth. I didn't mean it, but I wished I did. I wished I could be a stone-cold bitch. Wished I didn't turn into a mushy puddle every single time I saw him.

But I did.

I always did.

He was gorgeous. He was amazing and sweet and powerful. And I wanted him.

I wanted him so freakin' much.

But Jaxon had made his choice, and it wasn't me.

And that was exactly why I shouldn't go to the party. I didn't trust myself to steer clear of the demon, not on Halloween.

There was a second of breathless silence, and then Jaxon said, "Your sisters will be there."

That's because my sisters were over-sexed demon lovers. Not that I blamed them. Demons were excellent boyfriend material. Unlike warlocks, they were loyal, they were powerful, and when they picked a mate, it was for life. And Halloween was the night that most demons chose to mate. Actually, most found the call to claim their mate irresistible under a full Halloween moon, especially Hell's moon. The magic was just too strong to deny, or so I was told.

I smiled at him a little fuzzily; the effect he had on me was making me feel high. "Of course they'll be there," I said. "But I don't know if I should—"

He held up a hand, stopping me. "You should."

Silence. A really long, drawn out one, and then a

lazy, one dimpled smile split his lips that made my breath hitch and my lady parts tingle and pulse. "I brought you something."

I blinked, surprised, glancing down at his empty hands. "You brought me something?"

He nodded. "Hold out your hand, palm up."

I did. I couldn't help myself, and with a snap of his fingers, I suddenly had a pumpkin colored bag hanging from my palm. I glanced up at him, arching a brow.

"It's a costume," he said, and ran his hands over his hair. "I really hope you'll come tonight, Liv."

"I'll think about it," I heard myself say, feeling a pure burst of something that resembled panic, mixed with excitement. I clasped my hand around the bag handles.

More silence.

I stared at him.

He stared right back at me.

My stomach fluttered and my heart squeezed.

The line moved again; it was finally my turn to order. "Thanks for the costume, Jax. Maybe I'll see you later."

And then, I turned from him and stepped up to the counter, ordering my mocha.

2

Jaxon

MAYBE THE COSTUME WAS A BAD IDEA, BUT I'D WANTED
to make sure she knew I planned on getting her back,
and I'd figured bringing her something that
represented her favorite holiday might have helped
her remember that she was mine. She belonged by my
side.

But, yeah, the costume probably wasn't the way
to show her that. It definitely hadn't produce the
reaction I'd been looking for. I should have brought
her flowers, some orange and black roses.

No. Scratch that. I should have gotten her a
pumpkin. Liv loved pumpkins. Loved them almost as
much as she loved Halloween.

When she'd turned away to order her coffee, I
hadn't waited to see if she'd look in the bag, before
summoning a portal. Call me a coward, but given her
quick brush-off, I hadn't wanted to see any hints of

disappointment on her pretty face if she didn't like it. I didn't think I could handle it.

Hell was teeming with excited energy when I stepped through the portal into the Great Hall. My father's demons were everywhere, setting up for the party. The band was setting up on the stage. Chairs and tables were being set out. Decorations were being hung.

Nobody looked at me as I walked around the room. I went by the stage, and checked out the tables. Many of them already had centerpieces—a skull inside a cake plate with wilted rose petals scattered around the outside of the plate. *Perfect.* Liv would love them.

I moved from table to table, inspecting everything. This year we were going for a traditional mortal theme because, well, that's what Liv liked. Zombies, witches, vampires, tacky decorations. Fake spider webs hung in the corners, ghosts and bats hung from the ceiling. There were even a few skeletons and tombstones scattered throughout the room. But as I continued to scan the room, my smile faltered. There were no—absolutely no—pumpkins.

Panic coursed through me, seizing my ability to move. I wanted to make this the best Halloween party ever, one that Liv would never forget. And a Halloween without pumpkins ...

No. Not acceptable.

I had to do something.

Okay.

Okay, okay, okay.

Don't panic.

It was only a little after eleven o'clock in the morning. Plenty of time to get this fixed, and have everything ready before the party started.

"We need pumpkins," I shouted. "Big ones."

Fredrick, one of my father's advisors, scurried over to me. The short green-scaled demon looked up at me with questioning beady black eyes. He hesitated for about a second, just long enough for me to know he was surprised by my demand, then asked, "Pumpkins, sir?"

"Yeah, pumpkins," I said. "Replace all the chairs with big ass carved pumpkins."

"I don't think that's—"

"I didn't ask you what you thought," I said flatly, cutting him short. "I want this place to look like Halloween. And pumpkins—carved jack-o-lanterns—are exactly what we need."

Fredrick's face went blank—completely blank—except for his eyes, which shone with amusement. They all thought it was hilarious that I wanted a mortal style Halloween party. "Yes, sir," he said, and his voice was just as blank as his face. He hesitated for a moment, and then nodded, glancing around the room, a small smile curling his scaly green face. "I'm on it, sir."

And then he turned from me, barking out orders.

Well, I thought. *At least that's fixed. I just hope she shows up to see them.*

"Pumpkins aren't going to make her forgive you,

big brother." Suzie. I turned toward the sound of her voice. She was on the stage, staring at me. I hadn't noticed her there, but that was probably because I was thinking about the damn pumpkins.

She was right though. Pumpkins weren't going to make Liv forgive me, but damn, they might help make her temporarily forget how much of an ass I was.

My little sister dropped the power cords she was trying to untangle and hopped down from the stage, strolling toward me. She was already in costume. A princess, I thought, although she had her fangs extended. Maybe a vampire princess? I wasn't one-hundred percent sure. Her long dress was pink with white lace around the hem, collar, and sleeves, and she was wearing a sparkling, gem-filled tiara.

"I don't need her to forgive me," I said. I shoved my hands in my pockets and clenched my jaw. I didn't like talking about all the mistakes I had made with Liv, especially not with my sister. She was fifteen, still too young, and far too sheltered to really get it. "I just need her to give me another shot."

She laughed, but it sounded a little shaky and a little wrong, and she tucked a long strand of her dark brown hair behind her ear. "I'm surprised she agreed to come."

"She didn't," I said, a bitter bite to my tone. "She said she'd think about it."

Suzie nodded slowly as though she'd already known what Liv's response was, and then she smiled mischievously, flashing her fangs. "I might be able to help you with that."

I snorted out another laugh. "You can't help."

Suzie looked at me, blinked once, twice, then her expression shifted and she looked offended, although when she replied, her voice was cheerful, "See, that's why Liv left you. You're so bull-headed, never trusting anyone enough and never accepting help when you clearly need it. Trust me, brother. I can help you get her here. After that, though, it's up to you."

"Suzie—" I frowned at her for a second, and then shook my head. Shit. Was I really considering letting my little sister help me convince my girl to come to Hell? I sighed. Yep, I most definitely was. "Okay, fine, kiddo. What did you have in mind?"

3

Liv

I GLANCED AT THE SEXY WITCH COSTUME SPREAD OUT AT
my feet on my bed. It was mostly black. A black corset
with white floral embroidery down the center, a sheer
black lace skirt, and a black velvet witch hat.

I ran my fingertips along the soft brim of the hat. I
couldn't believe Jaxon picked this out. It was perfect.
Beyond perfect. It would cover me up, but still give
me a sexy edge, and a witch dressing up as a witch ...

Damn, I loved his sense of humor.

Add in some knee high black leather boots and a
swipe of deep red lipstick and the outfit would be
amazing.

And seeing the look on Jaxon's face when he saw
me in it would be even better.

My heart ached with how good it was to see him
today, and at the same time, how much it hurt. I'd
missed him so much over the last two months, but

I refused to be with a man who felt he couldn't be himself with me. It just wasn't ... healthy.

I'd met Jaxon just over a year ago now. It was on my first day of classes at Gates of Hell University. I'd bumped into him at Witches Brew—literally—and dumped my mocha all over his crisp white T-shirt. He'd taught me a spell that day, one that I've used many times since, to clean up the awful stain on his shirt, and I'd fallen fast and hard. He'd been so sweet, so charming, not to mention, such a good sport about my clumsiness, and everything had been good for a while—great, actually.

And then the truth came out, and all of his deceptions had ripped us apart.

But I still missed him. Missed him so damn much.

I froze at the sound of a soft knock on the door. I didn't go to answer it immediately, although I did turn to it. Taking a few deep breaths, I shook my head, trying to push away the memories of Jaxon, and listened, hoping whoever it was would just go away.

I didn't want to see anyone.

I didn't want anyone to see me.

The knock came again.

Sighing, I crawled off the bed, careful not to ruffle the costume, and went to the door, standing up on tiptoes to peek out the peephole. Suzie, Jaxon's little sister, stood there.

I opened the door.

Suzie was smiling, dressed up in the prettiest pink and white lace dress I'd ever seen. She grabbed me in a hug, and I rocked back a little from the impact. She beamed up at me when she stepped back. "Hiya, Liv."

"Suzie ... um, hey," I said, frazzled, and hastily stepped back, letting her come in. "What's up, sweetie?"

She came inside, closed the door behind her, and said, "Get your costume on. We're going to be late for the party."

I bit my lip and glanced at the clock. It was a little after nine. Then, I looked at the costume, indecisive. Goddess help me, but I wanted to go. I knew it wasn't a good idea, but I wanted to anyway.

After a moment, I gave her an apologetic smile. "Um ... no. I don't think I'm going to go."

Suzie's eyes turned from excited to concerned. She frowned. "What do you mean you're not going? It's the biggest bash of the year."

I settled for a shrug. I had no idea how to tell my ex's little sister that I couldn't go because every time I was around her brother all I could think about was jumping his bones. "I think I'm just going to stick around here and study."

"You love Halloween and you never study," she said. "You're avoiding my brother, aren't you?"

Okay, it was a little scary how quickly she nailed it. I fiddled with the edges of the skirt, straightening it out on the bed. "I'm not avoiding him. I'm just not in the mood to go to a party that he's at, is all."

"Right." She rolled her eyes. "You're not avoiding him at all."

I shot her a dirty look. "Jax put you up to this, didn't he?"

"Look ..." She bit her lip. "He misses you, Liv."

My eyes were narrowing, and I could feel my whole body coiling. I didn't want to hear it, didn't want to think about him missing me, because if I did, I'd think about how much I missed him, too. "Right."

"No." She walked across my room and plopped down on my bed, eyeing the costume. "He really does miss you."

Her statement made my heart stall, and then it raced. "He told you that?"

Frowning, Suzie eyed me peculiarly. After a long minute, she said, "Of course he didn't, but that doesn't mean I don't see it. He's a mess about the way things went down between you."

I let out a hollow laugh and it sounded a little cracked. "You know what? I'm not buying it."

"You know what?" she shot back. "I don't care if you buy it or not. It's the truth."

She shook her head and dropped her gaze, avoiding my stare.

I stepped closer to her. "Why are you here, Suzie?"

She didn't respond immediately, shifting her weight uncomfortably. When she finally spoke, her tone was ... sad, full of heartache. "I know what you must think of him," she whispered, "and I get why you're mad at him. I really do. But he loves you, we all love you, and I know you still love him."

I couldn't say anything to that, because she was

right. She nailed it again. I still loved him and I didn't think I'd ever be able to stop. I'd tried. Tried so goddamn hard. But it was useless. The thing was, I didn't think I could go back to how we were either. Maybe I could have, if Jaxon had have come clean sooner, but now …

When I didn't respond, she gave me a smile, a small, broken one. "Liv, please. Just get dressed and come to the party. You don't even have to talk to him if you don't want to. Just come … for me … please. I miss you, miss hanging out with you."

I walked toward my desk, bracing myself against the leather chair. I couldn't see why this was so important to her. I knew she loved her big brother, but it really wasn't like Suzie to get involved in his affairs. But she was doing a good job of making me feel guilty. Apparently, she knew that, because suddenly her hand was on my shoulder and she was holding the costume out for me.

"Fine, okay," I said, taking the skirt and corset she held out to me. "I'll go, but I'm doing it for you."

4

Jaxon

"WELL, I'LL BE DAMNED," DAD SAID FROM WHERE HE was seated beside me. "Suzie actually got her here."

I didn't look up from my drink. I couldn't. I'd felt Liv's presence the moment she walked through the portal, and I knew if I pulled my eyes away from my rum and blood cocktail, they would fly right to her.

"Yeah," I said flatly. "I didn't think she'd be able to pull it off."

"Well," Dad said. "What are you waiting for?"

It was a good question, but I didn't bother responding, not knowing how to answer it. I half expected her to come to me as soon as she arrived, but she didn't. It had been thirty minutes and as far as I could tell, Liv hadn't even glanced my way. My own relief startled me. As much as I loved her, I wasn't entirely sure how to fix everything.

I looked at Dad. He wasn't in costume, though he

was wearing his demon skin. Twelve-inch horns protruded from either side of his head, rough reddish-brown skin. His glowing green eyes shone at me, and what I saw there, I didn't like too much.

Pity.

I didn't want his pity.

All I wanted was my girl back.

"When you find a good one, you keep her," he said quietly after a moment. "Life's too short."

His statement made me laugh, because for a demon life wasn't short. Not at all. My gaze turned, searching out Liv. Most of the tables had been pushed aside, and the main area of the room was being used as a dance floor. People were pressed up against each other, swaying and gyrating.

I felt as though my body had been doused in gasoline and lit on fire as my eyes fell on her. Shit, she looked good in black and lace.

She was with Suzie and her sisters, a drink in her hand, leaning against one of the fake tombstones that were sporadically placed throughout the room. There was a demon there, one that was making her laugh, although I couldn't tell who it was. He was tall, at least six-feet, blond hair, and dressed like a pirate, his costume complete with a fake parrot on his shoulder.

My insides instinctively tensed when he leaned into her, whispering something in her ear, and then, he took her hand and ...

No way.

No fucking way.

I blinked, and then blinked again.

She was here for thirty minutes and she was already dancing with some other demon.

She wouldn't ...

She was ...

Gritting my teeth, I looked away, picked up my drink, and took a long sip. "She doesn't much look like she needs another man bothering her."

"You're right," he said. "She looks like she needs *her* man bothering her."

"I'm not her man anymore," I said, meeting his eyes. "I lost the upper hand in the relationship, and everything went to hell."

Sitting up straight, he pointed his drink at me. "Then take it back."

I hesitated. "It's not that easy."

"Sure it is," he said right away. "All you've got to do is walk up to her and tell her what you want and how it's going to be. She'll respect you for that, son, and if she doesn't, she isn't someone you want to be with anyway."

Silence fell. My gaze drifted from him, and fell back on Liv. She had her back to the demon, her ass, shaking and swaying.

Goddamn it!

She was mine.

Mine.

Her ass should be rubbing up against me, not the demon in the cheap pirate suit.

Was she trying to get my attention?

If she was, it was working.

Why did I always need to make her mine, stake my claim, every time I saw her?

She looked so fucking sexy in the sheer lace skirt, the pale white of her legs looking like porcelain.

My dick twitched.

And that corset made her breasts look huge, squeezing them together perfectly.

Another twitch.

Dad chuckled, and I tore my gaze away from her, settling it back on him. "Go on, son," he said. "If all else fails, just tell her you're sorry. Women love a good apology."

I stood up, grabbing and downing the last of my drink, and then walked away without saying another word to him, slowly making my way toward Liv. Everybody was dressed up, masks and make-up, the costumes ranging from the traditional zombies and vampires and ghosts, to well, some of them I didn't have a clue what they were.

Liv didn't hear me approach over the music, hadn't noticed me standing right by her as she dropped down, popping her ass back up against the demon she was dancing with. She seemed at ease, happy even, as she flirted and danced, a huge smile on her face. I wondered, uneasily, if it was an act, or if she was really having fun with the demon. It wasn't a pleasant thought.

"Mind if I cut in," I said loudly, nearly shouting over the music.

Liv stopped moving instantly, stumbling a little as she tried to straighten herself. She gave me a leery look, one the twisted my gut up in knots. I hated it. She used to look at me as though I was the only one worth looking at and now ... Now she looked at me as though she wanted to run.

"Um ..." She glanced behind her, frowning when she noticed her dance partner had backed off, and then looked back to me, shrugging. "I guess."

She looked a little less sure of herself, less ... edgy, as I stepped toward her, though still entirely way too sexy. She stood there, awkwardly shifting her weight from foot to foot as I placed a hand on her hip, pulling her against me.

"Jax," she said, looking up at me. She bit her bottom lip, and I was certain she was going to change her mind, but then she smiled, a sunshine bright smile, and said, "I love the pumpkin chairs."

And then, she started moving.

It was awkward and cute, the way her hips started to jerk from side to side. I slid my hand to the small of her back, tugging her tightly against me.

"So," I said. "Does this mean you forgive me?"

She let out a dry laugh and shook her head. "I'm here for Suzie, not you."

Her response made me chuckle. "I don't care why you're here, sweetness. I'm just glad you came."

Wordlessly, Liv stared up at me as she shimmied

and shook. I felt my dick harden with every jerky hip shake of hers. She felt so good against me. So goddamn right. And she smelled good, too. Like sunshine. Sunshine and lavender and mint.

Leaning down, I dragged my cheek against hers and said, "It's really not fair, you know."

Her head jerked back and her eyes widened as her hand flew up to my chest, pushing me back until she could meet my eyes. "What's not fair?"

"That you're mad about something I can't help," I said, keeping a firm hand on her back. Now that I had her body pressed against mine, I wasn't planning on letting her get away.

Her eyes widened even further, and she completely stopped moving. "I'm mad because you didn't trust me enough to tell me that you were the Prince of Hell. That's not really the kind of thing you hide from the person you're dating. I'm mad because you told me you loved me, but you lied to me about who you really were."

"You know what?" I said. "I didn't tell you because I knew this is how you'd react. I knew you'd make a big deal out of it. Knew you'd treat me differently. I trusted my instincts and it turns out my instincts were dead on."

The color drained from her face.

She knew I was right, but she didn't want to admit it.

She would never have given me a chance if she'd known who I was from the start.

I stared at her, surveying her face. Her expression was guarded, serious, but her eyes ... they couldn't hide the lust brewing in her soul. I could see it behind the pain, behind the anger, burning bright.

Leaning down, I pressed my lips to hers, kissing her lightly, testing. She didn't kiss me back, but she didn't pull away either. It only lasted a few seconds, before I let my lips drift, kissing along her jaw until I reached her ear. "Come for a walk with me, Liv."

"Jax ..." Her breath hitched, and then came out in a quick burst. "That's probably not a good idea."

"Probably not," I agreed. "But come with me anyway."

She gave me a peculiar look, one I'd never seen on her face before, and then said, "I—"

"We need to talk, Liv," I said, cutting off her protests. "You can't avoid me forever."

5

Liv

I WENT WITH HIM.

I shouldn't have. My head screamed not to. But I ignored it.

The moment his lips hit mine and I felt his hard cock pressing up against me, all my caution blew away on the wind.

I wanted him.

I needed him.

He stirred up something inside me on that first day we met, and that feeling had never gone away. Never faded.

It was intense.

It was intoxicating.

It clouded up my brain in a fog and made my heart skip and race.

Jaxon led me out to the gardens. The music was still pounding from the party, but it wasn't as loud out here. We moved through the rosebushes and past the gardenias, stopping at a fountain in the center.

He turned toward me once we stopped. The air was heavy with magic, and his black eyes shone bright under the crimson Hell moon.

He looked like he wanted to eat me up.

My heart hammered in my chest as he stepped toward me. "I've missed you, Liv," he said, his voice low and husky. "Why didn't you answer my calls?"

"Because you lied to me," I said, taking a hasty step back. "I don't have space in my life for liars."

He stepped toward me again and cupped my chin with his hand before I could retreat, tilting my face up so I had no choice but to look him in the eyes. His thumb swept along my cheek, and I let out a shuddering breath as he leaned in closer to me. "I've never lied to you."

My knees felt wobbly and so did my head. He was close. Too close. I could smell the rum on his breath, mixed with a hint of blood and mint. I couldn't think. I loathed the fact that his nearness could still do this to me. And when he leaned in even closer, and I felt the bulge in his pants pressing against me, I couldn't even breathe right.

Quickly, I pulled away, taking a large step back. "You did."

"What exactly did I lie to you about then?" he asked, arching a questioning eyebrow.

I rolled my eyes and huffed, frustrated, although I wasn't sure if it was from the conversation, or the way he had my body running hot with only a few touches. "Lying by omission is still a lie."

He flinched at my words, recoiling slightly as his eyes hardened and narrowed. "So your problem is that I didn't tell you that I'm going to inherit Hell someday."

"I don't care about what you're going to inherit, Jax," I said tightly. "I never did."

There was a tense, breathless silence.

And then he stepped toward me again, crowding my space. "If you don't care, then what's the problem?"

"The problem is you should have told me you were the Prince of Hell," I snapped, my eyes narrowing as I poked him in the chest. "What was your plan exactly? Claim me—mark me as yours—and then tell me? How do you think that would have played out?"

He reached out a hand, and I felt it brush against the bare skin between my corset and skirt, before he jerked my body back against him. "What does it matter?" he asked. "You loved me, still do love me. My title hasn't change that. I don't think there is anything that will change that, and I'm pretty sure you know it."

I squirmed, and then stopped when, once again, I felt his erection pressing against me. It felt good. Too good, sending tingles racing between my legs. Holy Hell. How was I supposed to stay angry when all I could focus on was how good it felt to have his dick pressed against me again?

I licked my lips, trying hard not to move. "Everything has changed."

"I can see it in your eyes, Liv," he said, clenching his jaw. "You love me. You hate it, but you do. You've loved me since that first day we met."

"Love at first sight doesn't exist," I scoffed, and then I lied to him. "It was lust, Jax. That's it. It was never love."

He didn't believe me. Not even for a second.

"It only takes four minutes to decide whether or not you're into someone," he said softly, barely loud enough to be heard over the pounding beat of music coming from the party. "It's been proven."

"Attraction isn't love."

He shrugged. "Semantics."

Silence.

His fingertips dug into my skin, holding me tighter against him. It felt so ... good. The warmth of his skin pressed against me.

"You could have told me, Jax." I dropped my eyes, looking down at his chest. "I loved you. Loved you so much it hurt. It wouldn't have mattered to me. You were the only thing that mattered."

"Stop it with all the past tense crap," he said, rocking his hips against me. "You still love me. I still love you. We still matter."

I shook my head, feeling very vulnerable just standing there with him so close. Reluctantly, I pushed against his chest, stepping out of his embrace. I felt the loss of his touch instantly. He didn't try to stop me, although the look in his eyes told me he wanted to.

"I can't be with a man who would hide things from me," I said. "I can't be with a man who doesn't trust me enough to let me into his world." I stalled for a moment, biting my bottom lip, and then sighed. "We should really get back to the party."

Jaxon cracked a smile, flashing a dimple, and said, "You don't really want to go back there. I'm pretty sure what you really want is to stay right here with me."

He was right. I did.

My skin was buzzing from his nearness, my brain was fuzzy, and my lady parts were pulsing with need. At that moment, I wanted nothing more than to be back in his arms.

Involuntarily, my eyes fell and I looked down at his hard length, straining against his jeans, remembering all too well what it felt like to have him inside me.

We'd been so good together.

So, so good.

I hesitated before slowly shaking my head, and then I lied, "Get over yourself, Jax. I don't want to stay here with you."

"I know you want me, baby. I saw you eyeing my dick. I bet your pussy is throbbing for me right now."

Dear Goddess. If I hadn't been feeling needy before, hearing him say that did the trick.

He took a step toward me again, but this time I took one back.

"Liv," he said, his voice low and husky. "Just let me have one more kiss. Please. Just one more. If you want to go after that, then fine. Go. I'll respect your decision."

I hesitated before slowly nodding my head. The truth was, I needed the contact just as much as he did.

And then his arms were around me and his mouth was on my neck. His lips were so soft as they travelled up, running along my jaw, before reaching mine. His kiss was gentle, just like the one he gave me on the dance floor. It took my breath away and I melted against him, letting out a soft moan.

"Tell me you don't feel that," he said, as he pulled back. "Tell me you don't feel the magic between us."

I didn't have the heart to argue with him, because I felt it, and I knew, deep down, he was right. No matter what my head said, my body and my heart were his. "I feel it," I whispered. "I'm feeling all kinds of intense with you. I'm not sure I should trust it."

A hint of a smile took over his face. "You should."

6

Jaxon

"Jaxon." Liv squirmed in my arms, trying to slip away, but I held tight. "We should get back to the party."

"Not until you realize that you're mine, Liv," I told her quickly.

"Jax." My name was strained as it came from her lips, and her breathing picked up, coming out in quick bursts. "You said you'd respect my decision."

"I love you," I said. "I've loved you from that first moment I saw you. I didn't tell you who I was because I was scared you'd run away screaming. I just ..." I stalled, carefully considering my words. "This is going to sound stupid, but I thought if I waited until you fell in love with me you wouldn't be able to walk away when you found out being with me meant you'd be bound to Hell for the rest of your life."

It was true. At first, I'd decided not to tell her about

my Prince of Hell status because I didn't know if she would stick around. Not too many women would, not even a witch like her. But then, as the time drew on, and I knew for certain that she was the one—my mate—I kept it from her because I wasn't sure how she would react after I'd hidden it for so long.

I still didn't know how she found out, although I suspected my father had something to do with it. But it wasn't really important. In the grand scheme of things, the only thing that mattered was that I wasn't the one who told her.

She narrowed her eyes and pursed her lips. "You're right, that does sound stupid."

"Please, baby," I said. "I need you. You're mine. You belong right here in Hell with me and you know it."

She glowered at me and it was so goddamn adorable. She was trying so hard to look tough, but I could see the emotion cracking her façade. It was in her eyes. They were soft and melty and warm.

Her lips parted, and I waited. Every muscle inside me tightened with anticipation, but all she gave me was a breathy exhale.

Shit. I needed her. Needed to feel her. Needed that connection.

I leaned down, kissing her cheek, her chin, her throat, my teeth nipping at her soft skin, hoping to Hell she wouldn't push me away again. Her skin was warm, flushed. She was feeling just as needy as I was.

I claimed her mouth then, my lips meeting hers,

hungrily, and to my surprise, she kissed me back. Hard. Her tongue pressed against my lips, urgently working its way into my mouth, and her hands gripped the back of my neck, jerking me closer.

"Tell me," I growled, ripping my lips from hers. "Tell me you're mine again. Tell me you'll forgive me."

I wanted to hear her say it.

Needed to hear the words.

She whimpered, her big eyes meeting mine. "I've missed you so freakin' much."

Something in her snapped then, something that I didn't quite understand. I saw it, though, in her eyes. The raw need. The confusion. The anger. It all mixed together, making her eyes brighten and almost glow in the moonlight.

She closed her eyes, her lips moving, forming silent words. I felt the magic she was summoning, and I held my breath. I didn't know what to expect, but when the veil snapped around us, hiding us from view, my heart rate picked up.

Her eyes opened then, and she grinned at me as her hands left my neck, going down to my belt, and she worked fast to get it undone. Shoving my jeans and boxers down enough to free my aching cock, she grasped onto it, pumping it once, twice, before looking up at me with hooded eyes. "Jax, please. I need you."

As it turned out, I didn't need the words. All I

needed was a sign, any sign that she was needing me as much as I was needing her.

Grabbing her thighs, I hoisted her up, taking a few long strides over to the shed, and pressing her up against it. Her magic followed us, the veil shimmering under the moonlight. She wrapped her legs around my waist, and I could feel her wetness as she ground herself against my dick. I pushed inside her, hard, thrusting deep.

It felt good.

So fucking good.

It felt ... like home.

Liv cried out, burying her face in my neck, and she bit down. She wasn't gentle about it, but she never was. She loved to be fucked hard and fast and I didn't hold back, going deeper with each thrust.

I fucked her the way I knew she wanted, gave her what she craved.

"Baby, you feel so good." I nipped at her ear, thrusting in and out. "Shit, I've missed this. Missed you."

"Don't talk," she said, her breath hitching. "Just fuck me ... please."

The wall of the shed groaned and moaned with each hard thrust. I kissed her again, hard. It was a desperate kiss, full of need and longing. Her hand dug into my neck, her nails digging in, and raking down to my shoulder.

Liv's hand slipped between us then, her finger

searching out her clit, circling and pinching and it didn't take long for her to start stiffening in my arms.

"Jax," she gasped. She was close. So close. I could feel it, feel her pussy fluttering around my dick. "I'm going to come."

She inhaled sharply and her breath left her on a moan as her orgasm hit. Her pussy clamped down on me, fluttering and convulsing around my cock. It sent me over the edge and I groaned, pumping in and out of her quicker and harder. I buried my face in her neck as it hit me, thrusting, once, twice, three times. A shiver ripped down my spine as I came, emptying my seed in her wet heat.

I stared down at her, soaking in her flushed cheeks—that just fucked look that she wore so well. Her eyelids were half closed, her head tilted, leaning against the shed.

Seconds passed. Five. Ten. Fifteen. Twenty.

All I could think about was claiming her, marking her so everyone knew she was mine.

Mine. All mine.

My fangs sharpened as I stared at her throat, wondering what my mark would look like there.

I knew the music was still pounding, but all I heard was our ragged breaths and thumping hearts.

I leaned down, brushing my lips against hers softly. "Liv, can I—?"

I didn't get a chance to finish the question. Placing a hand on my chest, putting pressure there as her gaze locked onto my fangs, she said, "Don't. Please don't ask that tonight."

I nodded wordlessly, as my chest constricted, a sharp crack spreading through my heart.

She stared into my eyes, breathless, as I slowly let her down. Straightening her skirt, her voice was low, nearly a whisper, when she said, "I need to go home."

"Liv ..." I stalled, raking a hand over my face. Shit. She looked like she was about to bolt. "Baby, stay, please."

She took a quick step back. "I need to think, Jax. I need ... time."

My first instinct was to refuse. I'd just bore my soul to her, and I didn't think I could let her go. Not again. But the look in her eyes told me I had to.

If time was what she needed, then I knew I had to give her that.

Hell, she'd already been gone for months, what was a few more days?

Wait. What if it took more than a few days?

I nodded once, summoning a portal for her, but I didn't say a word. I couldn't, because I knew if I opened my mouth, all that would come out would be pleas for her to stay.

She gave me a small, sad looking smile, and then she turned away from me, stepping toward the portal. She glanced over her shoulder as she reached it, surprising me when she said, "I love you."

Liv stepped through the portal then, disappearing

from my sight, and I snapped it shut, before I found myself rushing in after her.

7

Liv

I DIDN'T SLEEP A WINK THAT NIGHT. MY MIND WAS TOO
busy, and no matter what I did, it wouldn't turn off.
And after what just happened, the bed felt empty
without Jaxon beside me. I felt the void. I'd been
feeling it for two months now. The longing and
loneliness and heartbreak.

I tossed and turned, then paced and cleaned. I
scrubbed the floor, dusted my bookshelves. And the
night dragged.

And dragged.

And dragged.

I thought about Jaxon. I thought about the good
times we had—there were a lot of them. He'd always
been sweet to me, kind, always putting my needs
before his. And he could make me laugh at any time,
no matter my mood.

He was a demon, the Prince of Hell, and evilness

ran in his blood, but to me, he'd been nothing but good.

And I missed him.

The feelings hadn't faded even a little while we were apart. If I'd thought they had, last night had showed me how wrong I was.

But he'd lied to me. Hid things from me.

Oh hell, did it even matter? I was starting to feel like I'd overreacted about the whole thing. Maybe, just maybe, I shouldn't have gotten mad and walked away from him.

No. What I should have done was talk to him, because, as they say, communication is key.

By the time ten o'clock in the morning rolled around, my dorm room was spotless, and I was back in bed. I had my phone in hand and I was staring at his number in my contacts list when there was a knock at the door.

Setting down my phone, I threw back the covers and slipped out of bed, opening it. Jaxon stood there, dressed as usual in blue jeans and a black tee.

"Um, hey." I blinked, staring at him with shock. "You're using the door?"

My question made him chuckle. "I was told that's what normal people do."

"I ... um," I stalled, hesitating. "I was just about to call you."

Jaxon's smile was suddenly luminous. "You were?"

"Yeah, I ... uh ... I ..." I stammered, his smile, those dimples, and the fact that I'd never seen him use a door—ever—were throwing me off kilter. Finally, I nodded and stepped back, letting him in. "Yeah, um, come in."

He stepped toward me, reaching out and gently rubbing my arm as I shut the door behind him. "Are you okay, Liv? You look like you're run down."

"I'm fine," I said. "I just didn't sleep much."

He frowned at me. "Climb into bed."

I blinked at him. "What?"

"Climb into bed," he repeated. "I'll make you some tea."

I just stood by the door, wringing my hands together. We had sex last night, and although it hadn't been the first time, somehow it felt like it was. It had been rushed and clumsy. Desperate. And now, I was nervous. I didn't know what to say or what to do, but climbing into bed when my skin was heating and tingling just from the sight of him didn't seem like a good plan, at least not until I told him how I felt.

"I'm okay," I said. "Really."

He let out a laugh of disbelief as he stepped towards me. "Baby, I wasn't asking. Get that sexy ass of yours into bed."

I opened my mouth to respond, but I had no idea what I was going to say. It didn't matter, though, because he didn't let me speak. He scooped me up in his arms and carried me to the bed, laying me down and tucking me beneath the blankets.

I watched him, yawning, as he walked over to the small kitchenette, filling up the kettle and plugging it in. He didn't say a word as he pulled out a mug and slipped a tea bag in, waiting on the kettle to boil, and neither did I.

My stomach clenched from nervousness and my heart hammered in my chest as he poured the hot water into the mug and turned to me. I expected him to hand me the mug but he didn't, instead setting it on the nightstand, climbing up onto the bed with me.

He stared at me for a moment, swallowing hard. "So ... you were going to call me?"

"Yeah," I said, offering him a smile. "I was."

"Should I ...?" He hesitated, looking away from me. "Did I give you enough time to think?"

I nodded. "Yeah."

"Whatever you want," he said when I didn't elaborate. "I'll do whatever you want. Leave, stay, whatever."

My heart seemed to stop for a second. I wasn't sure what to say. His tone was so matter-of-fact, so unemotional that it made me freeze.

When I didn't respond, he took both of my hands in his.

"Liv, I'm sorry. At the time, I didn't see any other way, but I promise, I'll never keep anything from you again. Ever." Jaxon swallowed, his eyes fixed on me. "I love you, Liv. I don't want to be without you any longer."

"I love you, too," I whispered. And I did. I didn't always want to, but my heart didn't seem to understand that.

He kissed me then, and there was a lot of hunger and desperation in that kiss.

When he pulled back, his eyes shone, and that smile ... I just knew that everything was going to be okay.

I looked at him, a smile tugging at my lips. "I'm happy you're here."

"I'm happy to be here." He let go of my hands, grasping my chin, and pulling my face toward him. I exhaled shakily as he leaned in, kissing me softly and sweetly, over and over again. He pulled back for a moment, meeting my gaze and whispered, "Thank you for giving me another chance, baby. You won't regret it. I swear it."

And then he was on me.

His hands were gentle but quick as he tore off my nightshirt, tossing it to the floor. His movements were frenzied—frantic—setting my heart and body on fire.

My hands moved just as quickly, tearing off his shirt, and undoing his pants. I looked up at him, saw the heat in his eyes as I pushed him on his back and kissed my way down his chest. He was hard when I reached his cock. I wrapped my hand around his length and stroked a few times, watching him, before swirling my tongue around the head, tasting him.

He groaned.

His hands dug into my hair as I took him into my mouth. I kept stroking him with my hand, unable to take his whole length in my mouth, as I worked my lips over his velvety flesh, the whole time, keeping my eyes locked with his.

He stopped me not long after I started, tugging on my hair, until my mouth popped off his cock. "Climb up, Liv. Ride me."

I didn't hesitate, climbing up and sinking down on his shaft, and then I rode him. His hands were on my hips, guiding me, as I ground against him, popping up and down on his length. My hands were on his chest, my fingernails digging into his flesh, and I could feel his heartbeat racing against my palms.

It was ... amazing, feeling his life.

Leaning up, he captured one of my nipples in his mouth, sucking on it before nipping, as his fingertips dug into my hips, lifting me up and down, helping me move faster and faster.

I could feel it coming, the tension in my body, the coiling and tightening. I slipped one of my hands between my legs, circling a finger around my clit. It only took a few more seconds for me to shatter around him.

And then, just moments later, Jaxon followed me over the edge, groaning through his release.

I collapsed against his body then, lying there with his arms around me and my cheek on his chest. We were both quiet as we caught our breaths and waited for our heartbeats to return to normal, although after what felt like at least ten minutes, I wasn't sure if mine would ever slow down.

After a while, he kissed the top of my head, very lightly, and asked, "Will you be my forever, baby?"

Those words made my heart skip a beat. *Forever.* I liked the sound of that. I looked up at him, my smile so wide it hurt, and my head started bobbing up and down. "Forever sounds amazing."

Note from the Author

If you enjoyed *Halloween in Hell*, please consider leaving a review or rating on the site where you purchased it. Word-of-mouth is crucial for any author to succeed and your review, even if it's only a sentence or two, makes a huge difference in helping new readers make the decision to read my books. Many thanks for your support. It's very much appreciated.

XOXO,
Ashley Stoyanoff

Titles by Ashley Stoyanoff

THE SOUL'S MARK SERIES
The Soul's Mark: FOUND
Waking Dreams, A Soul's Mark Novella
The Soul's Mark: HUNTED
The Soul's Mark: BROKEN
The Soul's Mark: CHANGED

DEADLY TRILOGY
Deadly Crush
Deadly Mates
Deadly Pack

PRG INVESTIGATIONS SERIES
Two Truths and a Lie
Play It Again

OTHER TITLES
If I Could Do It Again
Halloween in Hell

About the Author

Romance author Ashley Stoyanoff is the recipient of two Royal Dragonfly Book Awards for young adult and newbie fiction. Her first book, *The Soul's Mark: FOUND*, came out in 2012. Her other passions include reading and shopping for the latest fashions. Learn more about Ashley and her work at ashleystoyanoff.com.